KU-265-206

This mini edition first published in 2008 by Andersen Press Ltd.
First published in Great Britain in 1995 by Andersen Press Ltd.,
20 Vauxhall Bridge Road, London SW1V 2SA.
Published in Australia by Random House Australia Pty.,
Level 3, 100 Pacific Highway, North Sydney, NSW 2060.

Colour separated in Switzerland by Photolitho AG, Zürich.
Printed and bound in Singapore by Tien Wah Press.

10 9 8 7 6 5 4 3 2 1

British Library Cataloguing in Publication Data available.

ISBN 978 1 84270 894 1

This paper is made from wood pulp from sustainable forests

I Want My Dinner!

Tony Ross

Andersen Press
London

"I WANT MY DINNER!"

"Say PLEASE," said the Queen.

"I want my dinner . . . please."

"Mmmmm, lovely."

"I want my potty."

"Say PLEASE," said the General.

"I want my potty, PLEASE."

"Mmmmm, lovely."

"I want my Teddy . . .

. . . PLEASE," said the Princess.

"Mmmmm."

"We want to go for a walk . . . PLEASE."

“Mmmmm.”

"Mmmmm . . . that looks good."

"HEY!" said the Beastie.

"That's MY dinner."

"I want my dinner!"

"Say PLEASE," said the Princess.

"I want my dinner, PLEASE."

"Mmmmm."

"HEY!" said the Princess.

"Say THANK YOU."